INKY

Nice neighborhood. Bad cat.

Chris Holmes

Other books by Chris Holmes
From Paranormalice Press, LLC

Light a Candle; Chase the Devil Away – 2019 Gold Medal Winner, Royal Palm Literary Awards

Vamped – The Turning

PARANORMALICE
PRESS, LLC

Books available: www.paranormalicepress.com, Amazon.com, and as ebooks on Kindle.

Sincere gratitude to author, mentor and friend, Veronica Helen Hart and the members of the Daytona Beach Writers Group and the Daytona Fiction Writers Group for their support, guidance and encouragement. Special thanks to William E. Dempsey, author, William G. Collins, author and Jean Cassidy.

Cover design by whiterabbitgraphix.com

Inspired by and dedicated to
our adopted feral cat,
"Mow"

INKY

Nice neighborhood. Bad cat.

Jim Harper breathed in the heady scents of freshly cut grass and tilled earth, the fruits of his day's labor. With his reward, a cold bottle of beer cradled in one hand, he settled into his rocking chair on the front porch and propped his feet up on the railing. His worn deck shoes framed the view of the charred, skeletal hulk across the street. It had once been the house of his best friend and neighbor, Bill Fuke.

Jim still shuddered at the memory. Bill and his wife, Nancy, lost their home in a tragedy the fire inspectors still couldn't explain. Unlike Jim's modest block home, theirs had been an old Florida two-story, wood-framed with a wrap-around porch. Three months ago it looked more like the gateway to hell with flames shooting over thirty feet in the air. A noisy fire, it had groaned and popped as it spewed billows of black smoke high above the tree line on the secluded cul-de-sac locals called The Little Hammock in Sago County, Florida. Thankfully, Bill and Nancy made it out unscathed and even managed to save Max, their ten-year-old Border Collie, before the inferno consumed everything else.

The houses on either side of the Fukes' lot stood abandoned with FOR SALE signs displayed. A realtor occasionally held open house events. The only other activity across the street occurred every couple of weeks when a man hired by the realty company showed up in white pickup and mowed the grass down to a respectable height.

The neighborhood had certainly changed in the thirty-three years Jim had lived there. He took a long swig of beer and then wiped his mouth across his sleeve. Tammy would fuss at him for doing it, if she were here, but she wasn't. The image of his manicured front lawn blurred as he thought of his deceased wife. Daylight dimmed and the chirp of frogs in the thick, surrounding woods heralded the coming night.

Jim's peaceful time of reflection ended abruptly at sunset, as usual.

Next door in Dora Pritchard's carport, a metal trash lid clanged and vibrated on the concrete pad, followed by rustling-paper noises. A bare, single light bulb swayed, sending shifting planes of light onto Jim's side yard. Other than the house on his left with the young couple who both worked nights, crazy Dora was his only remaining neighbor on the cul-de-sac.

Jim snorted. "No wonder I've taken to talking to myself."

The rustling sounds in Dora's carport stopped. Then he heard them. Off in the distance, soft mews mingled intermittently with the frog song. Soon low, wiry, shapes slunk from the dark underbrush of the woods at the curve of the cul-de-sac, then trotted across the road and converged around Dora's lit carport.

The meows, snarls and cries of the cats obliterated the melodic frog calls.

Dora's shrill voice greeted the gathering herd. "Here, kitty, kitty! There's my Cinnamon and oh, Bootsie and Tom-Tom. Bobtail, there's my good boy."

"Crazy old biddy," Jim muttered.

He lifted his feet from the railing and grimaced as blood flowed into his legs. Pins and needles stabbed his ankles and the prickly sensation hummed upward through his calves. Straightening in his chair, he craned his neck to peer around the bushy bougainvillea in his side yard and into Dora's cobblestone driveway. A spray of mulch flying out from his rose garden preceded the small calico who darted across his lawn to join the group.

"I just mulched that bed. Damn cats."

Dora tottered down her driveway, her skinny arms wrapped around a bulky shape nearly as big as she was. She adjusted her grip when she reached the sidewalk, bent at the waist and spilled what sounded like pebbles raining down onto the sidewalk.

Jim stood, tested his legs by rocking on his heels and then walked down the three steps to his front walkway.

"Jesus, woman. What in hell are you doing?"

Dora carried on her task in oblivion, cooing to the growing circle of noisy cats winding between her feet and rubbing their sinewy bodies against her calves. She tromped up her drive and returned a moment later hauling another open paper sack, which she dumped along the sidewalk as she inched her way backwards toward Jim's house.

"Dora!"

She turned, backlit by the wavering light in her carport, her cottony, white hair lifted in the humid breeze. She grinned, a pale, shriveled Jack-o'-lantern, with dark gaps outlining her crooked yellow teeth.

"Have you completely lost your mind?" The slap of his rubber soles on the sidewalk sent a ripple of fear through the swarm. The cats parted, some scampering a safe distance away into the road, others hunkering down in Dora's overgrown grass or crouching beneath shrubs, ears back and hissing.

"Oh, now Jim, hush, you scared 'em." She shook the

last crumbs from the twenty-pound bag over the sidewalk. Stray pellets bounced off the toes of Jim's shoes. "It's all right, babies. Mama won't let no one hurt yas. Come and get it, now."

Forty pounds of dry cat food formed a long ridge down the center of the sidewalk in front of Dora's house and ended just past Jim's fence line. Hunger overcoming apprehension, the cats crowded around the kibble buffet.

"Dora, you can't dump cat food on the sidewalk. You're just drawing more of these damn pests from the woods. What happened to the bowl you used to set out in your carport?"

"Jus' wasn't near big enough, Jim. Look at 'em all. They're starvin', poor things." She cracked open her mouth in another gap-toothed grin and peered up at him with too-bright eyes.

"Dora, this has to stop. Feeding one or two strays was one thing. But now you have," he paused and counted, "my God, there's at least forty of them!"

"They jus keep a comin'." She stooped to pet a gold-and-white tabby. The hem of her shapeless floral-print dress skimmed her scrawny bare shins, the skin on her legs a crosshatch of red scratches and dark scabs. "My ol' van's dead again. Would ya ride me to the store to get more food tomorra? I'm all out."

"Absolutely not. These cats keep coming because *you* keep feeding them. I'm sick of picking up cat crap and having my flower beds dug up and pissed on."

"Please, just one ride. I'll get the van fixed. They're God's creatures, Jim. I hafta look after 'em."

"More like the devil's creatures. Now, I'm asking you nicely to stop feeding them. If you keep on, I'm going to call animal control and have them set out traps."

She staggered back a step, one thin hand clawing at her neck. "Oh, no, no. Outta food. Hafta feed 'em." She wandered into the road, her fingers twisting tufts of her wild hair and pulling at her baggy sweater.

"Dora, listen to me. Feral cats carry diseases, fleas, ticks—God knows what else. And they're breeding like wildfire. I know you can't afford to take them all to a vet and have them fixed. Best thing is to just stop feeding them. They're hunters, scavengers—they'll survive."

Dora covered her ears and shuffled in a circle, her dirty, pink slippers scuffed against the blacktop. She grinned, stooped down and held out her arms. "Inky! Oh, Mama was so worried 'bout ya. Where ya been, boy?"

A black cat, sleek and lanky, strolled from the woods toward Dora. Several inches taller than the others, he held his head regally on an elongated neck as he strode past, ignoring Dora's outstretched hands. With the exception of one gleaming, lime-green eye, the rest of him disappeared into the deep shadows of the scrub oaks lining the curb. He emerged at the other end of the shadow and headed for the food.

Dora followed, beaming with pride. "That's my Inky. I call him that cause his fur's black and shiny as wet ink. Only has one eye, but he's a real smart one, he is. And look," she waved her bony hands, "he's been a busy boy."

Jim looked closer at the brood. The majority were pure black, like Inky. Though not as large, many had his angular face structure and long limbs. Inky was a busy boy, indeed.

"You didn't hear a word I said, did you Dora?"

Dora fussed over a small black cat with three white paws. "Hello sweetie pie, Mama's little Three Socks." The cat arched its back and purred as Dora stroked her fur.

A sudden shriek rang out. The cats scattered. Inky squared off with a mangy, gray male. The gray cat flattened its tattered ears and let out a menacing hiss. Inky countered with a deep, guttural growl, followed by a lightning-fast rake of his claws across the gray cat's face. Tail low, the gray male sprinted across the street and slunk off into the woods.

With his one eye focused on Jim, Inky crouched and scooped up a mouthful of pellets. Curved white fangs showed as he crushed the crunchy nuggets with his back teeth.

"Oh, Inky, why do ya hafta be so darn mean?" Dora turned and called to the other cats who cowered under bushes and behind tall weeds in her yard. "C'mon back and eat now. It's all right, darlins."

Jim pointed at Inky. "Trapping that one would go a

long way in lowering the feral cat population."

Inky stood, licking bits of kibble from his chops. He arched his back and lowered his head in a slow stretch. Then he launched his long body into the air. Blood bubbled in the deep scratches on Jim's bare shin even before the stinging pain registered in his brain.

"Ouch! That damn cat clawed me."

The cat ran off down the sidewalk, stopped a moment in the shadows and turned its head. One eye glowed in the midst of the blackness. Then it trotted off, blending seamlessly into the darkness of the underbrush at the edge of the woods.

"I'm bleeding like a stuck pig. Enough, Dora. If I see you feeding these vermin one more time, I'm calling animal control." He stomped down the sidewalk and shooed a gray-and-white cat from his rose bed before going into his house to tend to his bloody shin.

***

Early the next morning, Jim waited on his porch for his friend, Bill Fukes, to arrive for their weekly fishing trip. Their plan for today, a trip to Lake Crescent for freshwater bass. He checked his tackle box, cooler and the line on his rod. When the big, blue Chevy truck trundled up the street and parked, Jim picked up his gear and stowed it in the bed of the pickup, next to Bill's big red-and-white cooler and two camping chairs.

"Ready to catch the big one?" Bill asked.

Jim climbed into the passenger seat and closed the door. "Hope so." He rubbed the square tan patch on his shin, the largest available in the assorted-size box of Band-aids in his medicine cabinet. The deep scratches still throbbed. "If not a fish, then later on I'd like to catch me a big, black cat." He told Bill about his encounter last evening with Dora and the forty feral cats.

"Crazy ol' Dora. She's dumping food on the sidewalk now? Good Lord. When Nancy and I lived here, Dora acted a bit eccentric, but she only fed about a half dozen strays in her carport. They were always shitting in my flower beds and driving poor Max crazy with their damnable yowling at night." Bill shook his head. "Now it sounds like she's gone completely off her rocker. Does she still name them?"

"Yes. She christened the one who clawed me, Inky. A big, black, one-eyed tom. Fast bugger. Looks like he fathered most of the brood, too."

"Better watch out for cat scratch fever."

"I washed it good and then used an antibiotic ointment." Jim fastened his seat belt as Bill circled the cul-de-sac.

"Hey look, Bill said. "The old Conrad house has a sold sign out front."

Jim squinted at the sign as Bill rolled past. "Huh, that's new. That lady realtor had an open house there about two weeks back. Guess someone bought it. Hope it's a nice family. I miss you and Nancy. The neighborhood's eerily quiet with all these empty houses. Well, except for Dora and her damn cats."

Bill slowed as he passed the burnt-out wreckage of his former home.

"Still can't believe it's gone. Damned insurance company's dragging their feet. We finally got the Fire Inspector's report. They say the cause was electrical. Chewed wires in the attic." He shrugged and shook his head. "Their guess is squirrels."

"You had a new roof put on only two years ago. Shouldn't have been any access for squirrels."

Bill sighed. "Try telling that to the insurance company. I've lost patience. Nancy's dealing with them now. I just want it settled. I feel like a burden to Nancy's daughter, Lynne and her husband every day we stay in their house. Lynne's husband says at our age we're better off buying a condo and banking the rest. But I want a house. I'd like to rebuild right here."

***

Jim lightly banged his palm on the truck's tailgate, signaling he had removed his gear. Bill backed down the driveway. "Same time next Saturday?"

"Looking forward to it and my fresh bass dinner tonight, too."

Bill waved and gave a quick double horn tap and then drove away.

Jim opened the front door and walked through the

house to the back door. He unlatched the door on the screened porch that ran the width of the house, pattered down the back steps and around through the gate to the front yard. He picked up his fishing gear and the cooler containing the large-mouthed bass and carried it to the screen room. Normally he would have been disappointed catching only one fish the entire day, but the hefty weight of his prize made up for it. It would provide him with two thick, delicious fillets.

Plunking the Styrofoam cooler on his worktable, he spread out an old plastic tarp he kept expressly for the occasion. If Tammy were here, she would run off into the kitchen about now. Though she could make a tasty meal of any fish he caught, the act of gutting and scaling them made her queasy. After he cleaned it, he'd fire up the charcoal grill.

His fillet knife normally sliced through raw fish effortlessly, but tonight, as Jim made his first vertical cut down the fish's belly, he had to saw back and forth to cut the tough skin. A dull knife wasn't going to ruin his fillets. He laid the knife next to fish and walked into the house to retrieve his sharpening stone.

He heard a noise like a nail scraping on metal as he rummaged through the kitchen drawers. After listening for a moment and hearing nothing else, he located the stone and returned to the screen room. A long red smear on the beige tile floor caught his attention first. Next, the cut flap of screen on the door where the blood trail ended. He spun around. The bass was gone. Only his knife lay next to a small pool of blood on the tarp. He bent to examine the screen door. Two neat slices, one vertical and another horizontal formed a ninety-degree corner cut. The loose corner flapped outward.

A burglar cut his screen door to steal a fish? That didn't make sense, the cut was too small to allow entry, plus the door latch was still in the locked position.

He slid the latch open and stepped outside. Red splattered the white concrete steps, and something else. He squinted at the concrete in the late afternoon light. Paw prints. Bloody paw prints.

Scanning the back yard, he saw a large black shape leap from the roof of his garden tool shed over the fence and into Dora's yard. His prize bass dangled by its tail from Inky's mouth. Jim ran to the fence. Inky settled on a tree stump and tore out a hunk of the fish's belly. One defiant green eye glared at Jim as he chewed.

"Damn you, you little bastard!"

Jim marched through his side gate, across the lawn and up Dora's driveway. A few strays milled in her carport but ran off when he approached. He banged on her side door. No answer. He waited and banged again. The rattle of the glass jalousie slats proclaimed his anger. He stalked to the front door and jabbed the doorbell. No chime sounded. Everything about Dora's house looked as disheveled as she did, from the peeling pea-green paint to the unkempt, weed-choked lawn.

Jim gave up and skulked back to his house. He took the tarp and cooler into the back yard and hosed them clean, then walked the hose over to Tammy's flower gardens and lightly sprayed the beds. She loved the rock-bordered gardens he had created for her. She'd come home from teaching school, change into an old T-shirt and her favorite grass-stained Capris and spend the afternoons, weeding, pruning and planting. It relaxed her, she said. After she retired, she'd spent entire days puttering in the gardens. Her passion inspired Jim to create the big rose garden in the front yard. When he retired from the post office, they both spent the better part of their days working in the yard. Some days they simply sat enjoying the sunshine and watching birds gather around the birdbath, though over the years the visiting birds had dwindled. Probably due to Dora's cats.

He pulled the full length of the hose out to the smallest, farthest garden. A coquina boulder and an engraved stone plaque that read 'Cody' marked the grave of their beloved Golden Retriever.

"Hey, Cody. Miss you, boy. Can't believe it's been four years. You'd give that damn cat a good what for, wouldn't you?" Jim chatted with his old, best friend as he watered the fragrant lavender Tammy had planted around their dog's burial site.

Heading back toward the house, he rinsed the stone

birdbath in the center garden and filled it with fresh water. A short, stubby garden gnome holding a rusty metal lantern stood guard next to it. Tammy loved the silly gnome. She'd bought it for two dollars at a garage sale and named it, Chauncey. Jim chuckled a guilty laugh, remembering how upset she was the morning she discovered it missing. Six days later the first of a series of letters arrived with a photograph enclosed of Chauncey standing proudly beneath the Eiffel Tower.

He had given the little statue to Bill and Nancy to take along on their dream European vacation. Bill had a blast with the traveling gnome idea and snapped dozens of pictures of Chauncey at each site they visited. Tammy was so tickled, she made a collage of Chauncey's European tour photos and hung it up on the wall in her craft room. They hosted a barbecue for Bill and Nancy's return. Jim smiled, remembering how Tammy had kissed the gnome's cheek and then placed Chauncey back in his spot next to the bird feeder.

Jim bent to pluck a weed poking through the mulch at Chauncey's feet. Loud screeching from Dora's back yard startled him. He straightened up and peered over the fence. Inky and the big gray male were squabbling over the mangled, bloody remains of his beautiful bass. A slew of other cats darted around them, whipped into a frenzy, no doubt hoping for an opportunity to snatch a fishy morsel while the two males fought. Jim aimed the hose over the fence and turned the nozzle on. Shrieking, the cats dispersed, raced down Dora's driveway and disappeared into the woods.

"Good riddance, damned mangy devils." He rotated the nozzle to the off position. A low, rumbling growl came from Dora's yard. Gripping the hose, he searched for movement in the tall weeds. One lime-green eye peered from a diamond shape in the rotted lattice that covered the crawl space under Dora's house.

Jim turned on the hose full force and aimed the long jet of water into the lattice work.

"Take that, you one-eyed, fish-stealing sonofabitch."

***

At sunset that evening, Jim nursed his nightly beer and surveyed the deserted street in front of him. A peanut butter and jelly sandwich filled the gnawing hole in his stomach, but not his desire for grilled fresh bass.

"So peaceful," he mumbled. "Until Dora ruins it." The muted chirping of frogs echoed from the woods. Dora's house stood cloaked in darkness and overgrown shrubbery, not one cat in sight. It was past the time she usually fed them. Maybe the crazy old biddy heeded his threat after all. He leaned back in his rocker and enjoyed the summer night's breeze. It carried the sweet mingled scents of night jasmine and rose blossoms from his gardens.

***

The following morning, Jim stacked canned goods in

his pantry. "What an old fart I've become." On Sunday mornings, while most others attended church, he made his weekly trip to the grocery store, taking advantage of the nearly empty aisles. He even picked up the coupon circular at the front of the store like Tammy used to do. Saving a few dollars always made him happy. With the house paid off, his monthly pension and social security checks had kept him and Tammy comfortable. Any money he managed to save went into his fishing fund, a wide-mouthed glass pickle jar he kept on the kitchen counter.

But Tammy's prolonged illness and funeral expenses had wiped out their savings. He was forced to take out a second mortgage on the house, along with making hefty monthly payments to clear up the lingering medical bills.

He also cleaned the house on Sundays, or at least the few rooms he used. Piling his dirty clothes into a wicker hamper, he carried it into the laundry room next to the kitchen and started up a load of wash.

"Got my routine, all right." He plunked down into his recliner, levered up the footrest and turned on the television. Pressing the buttons on the remote, he hopped channels to a fishing show, a baseball game and then a golf tournament. After a late lunch, the hushed voices of the golf show's narrators combined with the steady hum of the clothes dryer lulled him to sleep in his chair.

***

He awoke after five in the afternoon, stretched and

headed out to water the gardens. "My routine," he muttered.

Though still early in the summer, the harsh Florida sun had wilted the more delicate plants. He picked up the hose and strolled across yard, letting it uncoil from its neat roll under the water spigot. When he reached the garden with Cody's gravestone, he turned on the nozzle. Out came a brief sputter of air, a spit of water and then nothing.

"Hmph, must have forgot to turn on the spigot." As he walked toward the house he heard the gushing water before he saw it. A foot down from the connection to the faucet, a torrent spewed out, soaking the block wall of the house and flooding the ground. Jim twisted the faucet closed and inspected the leak. A clean slice had nearly severed the hose. A few green nylon threads were all that held it from falling into two pieces.

"How the hell?" Dora immediately popped into his mind. The old bitch must have seen him spray the cats last evening, then snuck into his yard and cut his hose. Who else could it be? She's probably pissed I wouldn't take her to buy cat food. His only other neighbors he glimpsed occasionally, either coming in from or leaving for their work. He had no gripe with the young couple. But he did have one with Dora and her growing herd of feral cats.

The hose had cost over a hundred dollars, extra heavy duty and two hundred feet in length. A steady throb beat in his temples as he stomped around to the front yard and cut across the grass to Dora's house.

No matter how hard he banged on both doors, there was no response. He knew she was in there. She left the house but maybe once a week to go to the supermarket and stock up on bags of cat food. Her battered old white van with yellowed plastic taped over the driver's side window sat where she always parked it, in the tall grass on the far side of the house, so it wouldn't hinder her feeding the cats. He pictured her crouched on the other side of her front door with her gnarled fingers clamped over her gap-toothed grin and those pale, blue eyes glowing like two LED lights in her wizened head.

"That's it. I'm calling the sheriff." He strode back to his house.

**

Though he knew Sago County had a small Sheriff's Department, the forty-five-minute wait for a deputy to show up irked him. He had purposely traded his nightly bottle of beer for a can of ginger ale, so the deputy wouldn't smell alcohol on his breath and label him a drunk.

He rocked in his porch chair, not for relaxation, but in rhythm to his agitated state of mind. The more he thought about Dora slashing his garden hose, the faster he rocked. And that damn black cat stealing his fish. How the hell it managed to carry off a six-pound bass by the tail fin so easily still baffled him.

A sheriff's cruiser finally ambled down the cul-de-sac and parked. Jim hurried down the steps and then paced the sidewalk while the young man in the car talked on the radio and then shuffled through papers on the passenger seat. He finally slid from the car holding a notepad and looking bored.

"You James Harper?"

"Yes, deputy. Call me Jim."

The young man nodded. "I'm Deputy Rollins."

Jim led him through the side gate to the back of the house to examine the hose. The deputy's languid pace exemplified the low priority status he assigned to Jim's complaint. If Jim hadn't gotten himself so worked up about Dora's audacity to destroy his property, he might have agreed.

"Looks like it was cut all right," the deputy said. He scribbled in his pad and then pulled a flashlight from his belt. He swept the beam across the back yard. "Nice gardens. Are your fence gates secure?"

"Standard slide latches on both, no locks," Jim said. "It's a quiet neighborhood. My wife and I installed the fence to keep our dog in the yard. We weren't thinking about keeping vandals out."

"Might want to look into getting some locks." The officer flipped his notepad shut. "Well, give us a call if you see any suspicious activity, Mr. Harper."

"That's it? You're not going to question Dora?"

"Without proof or an eyewitness—"

"This had to be her retaliation for me hosing down her

cats."

"Hosed her cats? Sounds like animal cruelty."

"I didn't hurt them, just chased them. They're feral cats. At least forty of them. She feeds them—dumps two twenty-pound bags of cat food on the sidewalk every night. One of the damn things slit my back screen door and took the fish I was cleaning right off my work table."

"You witnessed this?"

"Not all of it, but I saw the bloody trail where it dragged the fish off, the cuts in the screen door." Jim pointed to the side yard where the tool shed stood against the wooden privacy fence. "I saw the cat carrying my bass in its mouth by the tail fin. It jumped from my shed roof over the fence and into Dora's back yard."

The deputy sighed. "Let's see the screen door."

They walked the few feet to the back-porch stairs and Jim pointed to the door. "Haven't had a chance to fix it yet."

The young deputy leaned closer, aiming his flashlight beam at the door as he fingered the cut edges of the screen. "You say a cat did this? This is fairly heavy mesh. Looks more like a cut from a razor knife."

"I didn't see the cat claw the screen . . . unless . . ." a thought formed in Jim's mind, "maybe Dora cut the screen to let the cat inside?"

The deputy wrote in his notepad. "This Dora, she ever give you trouble before? You know, trespassing or climbing over your fence?"

Jim chuckled at the image of scrawny, old Dora scaling the four-foot high cedar wood fence. "No sir, I think Dora's fence climbing days are over. She's got to be in her eighties, hell, maybe nineties. Looks about a hundred."

"Sounds like cutting that thick garden hose might be too much of a chore for an elderly woman."

"Oh, she's spry enough. Hauls around twenty-pound bags of cat food every night. And she could have simply opened the gate, walked into the yard and cut the screen door and the hose. I refused to give her a ride to buy cat food. And I threatened to call animal control and report the feral cats. Probably what set her off. She loves those damn cats."

The two walked around to the front of the house. The deputy continued on toward his patrol car.

Jim called after him, "Deputy, would you talk to her at least? Maybe having the law show up at her door would be enough to scare her into not trying any more stunts." Jim's shoulders slumped and he let out a long breath. "I'm on a fixed income, with medical bills to pay. A new garden hose and screen for the door is expensive. I can't afford any more vandalism."

Rollins released the door handle of his cruiser. "Well, feeding forty feral cats in a residential neighborhood is illegal. I could issue a warning."

"Please. I would appreciate it."

"All right." The young man removed his hat, ran his

hand through his slick black hair and then placed it back on his head. "I'll talk to Dora—what's her last name, do you know?"

"Pritchard," Jim said.

Nodding, the law man strolled toward the dark, dilapidated house.

Jim followed a few paces behind the deputy and stopped at his fence line.

The deputy played the flashlight beam over the uneven cobblestones of Dora's driveway and then headed across the trampled trail of weeds leading to her front door. He rang the bell.

"Doorbell doesn't work," Jim called out.

The deputy pounded on the front door. "Ms. Pritchard! Sago County Sheriff's Department. I need to speak to you, ma'am."

Not receiving a response, he picked his way through the tall grass and then under the carport roof to the side door. The glass louvres shook when he knocked and called out again.

He walked back to Jim, who now stood in Dora's driveway.

"Appears Dora isn't at home."

"She's got to be. Her van's over there, though it's broke down, again. But she never has any company come by or take her out."

"When's the last time you saw Dora, Mr. Harper?"

"Night before last, when she was feeding the cats."

"You said she feeds them every night, but you didn't see her last night?"

Jim thought for a moment. "No, I thought maybe she listened to me and stopped feeding them."

"What time does she usually feed the cats?"

"Right at sunset."

"It's dark now. She's either late or she stopped feeding them, or. . ."

"Or?"

"How old did you say she was?"

"My guess is mid-eighties, maybe older."

The young man nodded, walked a few steps away and spoke into his radio. "Rollins here. I'll be conducting a wellness check at number 6 Briarwood Circle. A Dora Pritchard."

A voice obscured by static responded. The deputy aimed his light and high-stepped through the weeds around the back of the house.

Jim waited in Dora's carport, his hands in the pockets of his cargo shorts and rocked on his heels. A pang of guilt hit him. He never considered Dora might be ill or perhaps had fallen and was injured. Here he was bitching about a garden hose and she might be laid up in a dark house with a broken hip or worse for two days now.

He lifted the lid off the metal trash can where Dora stashed the bags of cat food. Empty. She really was out of food. She must have cut the hose out of spite and now hid sulking in her house. Hearing the deputy's footsteps crashing through the underbrush, he replaced the lid.

Once the deputy cleared the corner of the house, he spoke rapidly into his clip-on radio. "Going to have to force entry at 6 Briarwood Circle. No one's answering, but a neighbor is certain the elderly resident is at home."

He ignored Jim and hurried past him to the front of the house. His flashlight beam swiped the old oak branches overhead for a split second illuminating long, bristly, gray drapes of Spanish moss dangling in the air. Then, the distinct crash of breaking glass rang out.

Jim rushed to the front door as the deputy knocked the remaining shards from the window frame with the butt of his flashlight.

The young man tried reaching one arm inside the window, but a stack of magazines blocked his arm. He shoved the pile over and stuck the upper half of his body through the window in order to reach the front door. The lock clicked. After extricating himself from the window, he pushed the door, but it only opened halfway. A dank odor of mold drifted outside. The deputy aimed his light and squeezed through the opening.

A loud crash followed by a spew of curse words alarmed Jim. "Are you all right?" he called. He pushed against the front door, but newspapers stacked from floor to ceiling prevented it from opening further. The deputy exited, coughing and brushing his hands over his uniform.

"Tripped over something. Place is full of junk and the mold is pretty thick in there. I don't have a mask in my car either."

"I have some disposable masks. Use 'em when I fertilize. I'll get you one."

Jim hurried off to his shed and returned with two masks plus his heavy-duty flashlight. He handed one mask to the deputy and slipped the other over his face. "You think Dora's hurt?" he asked.

The deputy nodded as he secured the white filter mask over his mouth and nose. "I found an open window with a cut screen at the back of the house. Couldn't get in, too much stuff blocking the opening and too small a space to climb through. I shone the flashlight inside as best I could. Heard sounds but couldn't see anything."

The young man took a deep breath and then edged though the front door.

Curious, Jim followed without an invitation.

"You should wait outside until I make sure the house is secure," the deputy said.

"I doubt this is a crime scene, deputy. An extra light might be a help."

The young man shrugged and moved slowly through the maze of junk surrounding them. Piles of dusty furniture, cardboard boxes and plastic bins leaned precariously on either side of a narrow pathway. The path narrowed here and there, forcing the men to turn sideways to get their bodies through the tight spaces.

Jim followed, swiping his light side to side and up and down, amazed and appalled at the walls of trash looming around them. The path ended in a kitchen, non-functional, with heaps of rags and dirty dishes piled in the sink and trash obscuring every surface. The room smelled like sour milk. Jim turned to follow the deputy and his shoulder collided with something hard. A rusty toaster crashed to the floor.

"You really shouldn't be in here, Mr. Harper. It's not safe."

"I'm fine, deputy." He pushed the toaster aside with his foot. "Hate for you to wade through this mess alone."

"It's my job."

Jim noted the young man still hadn't ordered him to leave, so he continued to shuffle along behind the deputy's silhouette, their flashlight beams slowly sweeping side to side in front of them, illuminating mounds of clothes, stacks of newspapers and hulking piles of unidentifiable clutter. The hot, humid air reeked of mold. Dust particles swarmed in the beams of light like thick clouds of gnats. They squeezed through a tiny opening in the wall of junk and found a dark, equally cramped hallway that led to the rear of the house.

Cans, bottles, bloated plastic trash bags and still more newspapers towered above their heads. "Why would anyone keep all this shit," the deputy muttered. "Man, it reeks in here. Be careful, Mr. Harper. If you see a light switch, hit it."

"I don't even see a damn wall, much less a switch plate." Jim stopped. "What's that noise?"

Smacking sounds, like lips sucking juicy meat from a bone came from a darkened doorway just as the putrid odor of rotten meat assaulted Jim's nostrils beneath the mask. His stomach reacted with a rolling swell, sending a gush of acid partway up his throat.

The young deputy's voice cracked as he called out, "Ms. Pritchard?" He lowered his flashlight and aimed it inside the murky black opening.

Jim also trained his light into the dark room. He gasped at the sight of glowing eyes, neon red and yellow, caught in the rays of light. Too many pairs to count. Then, dozens of cats rushed the doorway. Sleek bodies pushed and squirmed between Jim's bare calves as the horde fled the room.

A dim light flicked on overhead. "Holy Mother," the deputy rasped. He held onto the wall where he had found the switch plate and stared down at the sight on the floor, then pushed past Jim and bolted out the doorway. Jim heard him gasping and retching in the hallway, but he couldn't pry his feet from the dirty carpet or force his gaze from Dora's mutilated body lying on the floor.

Dora's right hand, or what was left of it, wriggled.

Shiny white bones protruded where fingers had once been, the ragged chewed flesh at her knuckles oozed rivulets of blood onto the filthy blue carpet. Her face, a red-and-black concavity of shredded tissue and coagulated pulp held one pale blue eyeball. It stared up at him. Bubbles formed and a spray of red spewed from a deep, black hole above her neck. She gurgled, "Jim . . . you . . . hafta . . . feed . . . 'em."

"My God. S-she's alive," Jim turned toward the hallway and yelled. "She's alive!"

The deputy's sweaty, ashen face peered around the door frame. "Are you nuts? She's gone. Been dead a while from the stench."

"B-but she moved. She spoke. Didn't you hea–"

Rollins shook his head and ducked back into the hallway. Jim heard him radio for backup.

Dora's hand lay still now. One blood-smeared finger bone pointed directly at him. Good God, did I imagine it? I could have sworn she moved, talked.

A long, black shape leapt up from the corner behind a bed and onto a pile of boxes near the windowsill. Startled by the sudden flash of movement, Jim staggered backward, one hand clamped hard against his chest as if to prevent his pounding heart from bursting through his rib cage, the other aimed his flashlight.

With one blazing green eye fixed on Jim, Inky perched atop the stack of boxes and methodically licked blood from his front paw. A satisfied grunt accompanied each rasp of his tongue. The four extended claws from his raised paw cast a shadow of elongated curved scythes on the wall. The cat ran his tongue over his muzzle, then turned and shimmied out the narrow window opening and cut screen.

***

Jim handed the deputy a glass of ice water and then sipped from his own. The young man sat on the hood of his cruiser, shoulders hunched forward and nodded his thanks. With his face drained of color and a lock of black hair falling over his forehead, he looked more like a scared teenage boy than a sheriff's deputy. Jim forgave him for his earlier cockiness.

The ambulance crew had left after only spending a brief time inside the house. Now a shiny black coroner's truck sat parked in front of Dora's house.

An older officer, stocky and broad-shouldered, strode down Dora's driveway. He stopped and frowned at the young deputy. "Rough one, hey Rollins? You doing all right?"

Rollins's Adam's apple moved up and down. He nodded.

The older man stuck his hand out to Jim. "Sergeant Monahan. You the neighbor?"

"Yes, sir. Jim Harper. Live next door." Jim nodded toward his house as they shook hands.

The older man sighed. "Crazy ol' bat, that Dora."

"Did you know her?" Jim asked.

"Of her." He adjusted the broad-brimmed hat on his buzzed gray hair. "I was called out here about two years ago, by the family across the street." He pointed to the house with the SOLD sign. "The Murrays. Their four-year-old boy was mauled by cats. Hurt pretty bad. When I questioned her, Dora defended those cats like they were her kids." He jerked his head toward Dora's house and snorted. "Look where it got her."

Jim recognized the name when Monahan said it. "Yes, I remember now—the Murrays, husband, wife and their little boy. Um, Justin. They were always calling the boy's name to come in from playing. He liked to ride his tricycle around the cul-de-sac. Good kid." Jim took a long drink of water. "It was just about two years ago when they up and moved out. I don't think they had lived here more than six months. Then the Conrads moved in. They didn't stay very long either."

The three turned as uniformed men rolled a zippered, black body bag strapped to a gurney down Dora's bumpy driveway and then loaded it into the coroner's vehicle. A trick of all the revolving lights from the patrol cars probably, but Jim could have sworn the bag writhed under the straps as they lifted the gurney. A chill ran down his back despite the warm, humid air.

***

Jim finally dropped into his recliner after one in the morning. He craved a cigarette even though he had quit smoking twenty years ago. After toying with the idea of driving to the 7 Eleven to buy a pack, he flicked on the television instead and then immediately muted the volume. His ears pricked at every sound in the house—the refrigerator motor cycling, a random soft pop of the house settling, and his own elevated heartbeat. Tomorrow morning he'd go to Home Depot and get the materials to repair his screen door. He'd check all of his window screens. The thought brought little comfort. There hadn't been a thing wrong with his back screen door until that damn cat sliced it. Inky, the big black, one-eyed cat that licked Dora's blood from its paw. Was that the price Dora paid for not feeding the cats? If he had taken her to buy cat food would her death have been prevented? He shivered and yanked down the afghan draped over the headrest of his recliner. He spread it over his body and clutched it tight under his chin. Normally he'd turn off the AC and open his bedroom windows at night to enjoy the ocean-cooled cross breeze. It saved on his electric bill. Tonight, he kept the air conditioner running and all the windows shut and locked.

***

He awoke at sunrise after a fitful night of short naps peppered with vivid nightmares of Dora's lone blue eye and the raw black hole of her mouth gurgling blood. After a shower, he dressed to go to Home Depot. Instead, he sat hunched over the kitchen table sipping coffee with no appetite for breakfast or ambition to leave the house.

Uncharacteristic noises came from the road out front. He walked to the living room and peered through his blinds. A large U-Haul truck lumbered up the long gravel drive of the old Conrad house next door to Bill's old lot.

A smaller dark green pickup idled in front of Dora's house with ANIMAL CONTROL printed in white letters across the tailgate, and in the bed, stacks of cages. Ironically, Dora's death must have prompted the action. A husky young woman with short blonde hair and a green uniform exited the truck. She carried two cages at a time and placed them between the woods at the bend of the cul-de-sac and Dora's front yard. After making three trips, she returned to the truck and retrieved a bag, then walked back to the traps. She crouched by each, baiting and setting them. Once satisfied with her work, she drove off.

Moments later, two more pickup trucks sped down the cul-de-sac past Jim's house, rounded the curve and parked haphazardly in front of the old Conrad place. Loud music and the deep thump of bass notes emanated from one. Even with his windows closed, the heavy beats vibrated inside Jim's chest.

"What the hell is going on over there?" he murmured.

The music cut off with the engine. From the two trucks, five young men in jeans and T-shirts climbed out, slammed the doors and then sauntered across the lawn to the U-Haul. A sixth man, taller and sandy-haired, jumped down from the U-Haul's cab.

"So much for my quiet neighborhood. Looks like it's going to shit." Jim shook his head and gathered up his wallet and keys. Taking his time, he surveyed the scene across the street as he climbed into his SUV to drive to Home Depot. He cruised slowly around the curve and past the Conrad house. The back of the U-Haul stood open and the six men carted an oversized-brown leather sectional shoulder-high toward the open front door. They marched in unison, like ants hauling off a giant chocolate bar.

***

Three-quarters of the truck's spacious interior had been emptied by the time Jim returned home. Stacks of cardboard boxes filled the remaining space. The young men across the way sat on their open tailgates talking loudly and eating from white paper take-out bags. The tall sandy-haired one raised an arm above his head and waved to Jim.

Jim waved back then gathered up his purchases and carried the bags up his porch steps.

"Hey, how ya doin'?"

Jim turned, his key inserted in the front door lock. The sandy-haired man stood on his walk. He looked even taller up close, with tattooed, muscular arms extending from a sweat-stained, sleeveless, white T-shirt.

"Hello there. You my new neighbor?" Jim asked. He put the bags down outside the front door and climbed down the front steps. He stopped on the last step so he could stay near eye level with the young man and extended his hand.

"Yup. Name's Pete. Pete Driscol." He clasped Jim's hand in a tight squeeze.

"I'm Jim Harper. Good to meet you, Pete."

"Couldn't help but notice your yard. Place looks like a freakin' magazine picture. Who's your landscaper?"

"Thank you." Jim chuckled. "Can't afford a landscaper. I'm retired, so I have the time and, God willing, still have the energy to do the work myself."

"I used to do landscaping. Now I'm a contractor. Apex Construction." He fished in his back pocket and handed a creased, damp business card to Jim.

Pete pointed at Dora's house. "Hey, the realtor said the old lady in that house just died. Know if her family's selling it? Looks like a great flip house."

"Flip house?"

"Yeah, ya know. Buy it cheap, fix it up, sell it for profit. I'm always looking for a good flip."

"I don't know anything about the house." A cold, clammy tingle seeped down Jim's spine when he looked over at the shabby, deserted house. He cleared his throat and pushed away the vision of Dora's ravaged corpse. "Looks like a whole crowd of you moving in over there. You college boys?"

Pete snorted. "I'm thirty-four, Jim. Never went to college. Those are just some of my drywall guys helping me move. It's just me, my wife, Wendy, and our daughter, Emma." He grinned exposing a narrow gap between his front teeth. "Plus, a baby boy on the way."

"Huh, older I get, the younger everyone else looks. Well, welcome and good luck to you and your family." Jim smiled, turned and started up the steps. He stopped when Pete continued to talk.

"We moved down from Jersey a few months ago. Wendy fell in love with the house. Price was right. It needs some work, but I can do it all myself for pretty cheap. Turn it into a real showcase for my company." Pete smacked a pack of cigarettes against his hand, drew one out with his lips and lit it. It bobbed up and down as he talked. "We figured a cul-de-sac would be safer for the kids. This is a real quiet neighborhood." He grinned at Jim. "Not much excitement around here I guess, huh Jim?"

***

Pete proved to be quite a talker and a braggart, too. Jim chalked it up to his youth and a need to impress. He finally escaped from Pete's monologue by telling him he had to fix his back screen door.

Before attacking the screen door project, Jim fixed himself a bowl of cold cereal. He stood in the living room holding the bowl as he ate and peered through his open blinds at the activity across the street.

Pete pulled down the big rear door on the empty U-Haul. After more loud talking and laughing, the U-Haul and both pickups started up. Silence fell over the cul-de-sac as the last truck rumbled away. Jim would have to wait and see what kind of neighbor Pete turned out to be. In the meantime, he looked forward to hearing children playing on the cul-de-sac again.

His Tammy wasn't able to have kids. Instead she lavished her abundant maternal instincts on a new crop of third graders each school year. Jim had often wished for a son or daughter, but never voiced his wish out loud to anyone. It would have broken Tammy's heart.

***

He replaced the torn screen in the door with a new one and then screwed a neat square of heavy-gauge wire mesh over the bottom door panel. The only way Inky or any animal could get through would be with a pair of damn wire cutters. He planned to buy an entire roll of the heavy gauge mesh when his next checks came in. He'd reinforce the bottom two feet around the entire room. After sketching out a diagram of the screened porch, he carefully measured the perimeter and wrote down the measurements.

The repairs and measuring took up the entire afternoon. With his stomach still unsettled after last night's events, Jim ate a handful of crackers for dinner and then headed outside to water the gardens.

He wound duct tape around the cut hose and then turned on the water. The tape held. The temporary fix would have to do until he could afford a new hose. He walked to the end of the yard, dragging the hose along with him. More than once he heard something moving in the overgrown brush in Dora's back yard. Hair prickled on the back of his neck with each intermittent rustle. He swiveled around, expecting to see glowing eyes watching him from the long shadows, but saw nothing. He finished watering and hurriedly rolled up the hose.

***

He had just settled into his rocker on the front porch and twisted open a beer when a big black Ford F-350 hummed past his house, followed by a compact blue sedan. Pete waved, rounded the bend and pulled into the drive of his new house. A young woman steered the blue car into the driveway and parked next to the truck.

Pete hopped out of his truck and then helped a petite, very pregnant woman from the car's driver's seat. He leaned into the back seat and emerged holding a little girl, her small arms wrapped around his neck.

Jim rocked and sipped his beer as the three disappeared into their new home. The happy domestic scene made him miss Tammy even more. Restless, he put down his beer, pulled the pruning shears from the hook on the railing and busied himself clipping off the spent rose blooms. He made a neat pile of the cuttings on the front walkway to add to his compost box.

He jumped and cried out when a hand slapped his shoulder. Whirling around, he found Pete standing behind him sporting a toothy grin.

"Didn't mean to scare ya," Pete said.

Jim's heartbeat vibrated in his eardrums. "What can I do for you, Pete?"

"Wendy and I wanted to invite you over for dinner." Pete swung his big arm and pointed across the street. "Just pizza, nothing fancy. Probably be living on take-out for a while till we get settled."

"Oh well, thank you. But no, I—"

"C'mon, at least come over for a beer. I know you drink." Pete winked and jabbed his thumb in the direction of the empty bottle perched on the railing. "I want you to meet Wendy. She's due any day now and nervous about being alone while I'm working. It'd make her feel better if she at least met you."

Jim looked past Pete. A round patio table and four chairs had been set in the front lawn of the Driscols' house. Wendy carried a large pizza box from the truck's cab and placed it on the table. The little girl jumped up and down, squealing, "Pizza! Pizza!"

"I suppose. Just a quick hello. I don't want to intrude." Jim laid his pruners on the railing and followed Pete across the street. The spicy aroma of pepperoni made his stomach rumble.

***

Jim smiled and shook his head when Wendy offered him a third slice of pizza. He still munched on the crust from his second slice. Pete plunked a cold beer down on the table in front of him. The family, especially Pete's wife, had immediately made him feel welcome. Wendy turned out to be a soft-spoken young woman with a warm smile and a light, melodic laugh that reminded Jim of his Tammy. She doted over little Emma, wiping sauce from around the child's mouth with one hand while she clasped her pregnant belly with the other.

Pete's loud talk and macho swagger also faded in the blissful family setting. Jim liked this side of Pete as he observed how he helped Wendy into a chair and retrieved an iced tea from a cooler for her.

Emma never stopped scampering around the yard. She had her mother's wide brown eyes and her father's thick, sandy blond hair pulled into two ponytails that stuck out from either side of her head and bounced as she ran. Pete cut open a box of toys in the house and she ran back and forth giggling as she brought out a toy, showed it to Jim and then raced inside to snatch another.

Wendy stood with a soft groan, supporting her back with both hands. "Time for bed, Emma."

Mischief curled the little girl's lips. She dashed across the yard towards the woods.

Jim jumped to his feet. "No, sweetheart. Don't go near the woods!"

Pete loped across the lawn in a few long easy strides and caught Emma up in his arms. She squealed when Pete tossed her into the air and then caught her.

"Bad cats in those woods," Jim muttered.

With Emma riding on his shoulders giggling, Pete jogged back to the table.

"Good move, Daddy. Now she's ready for bed." Wendy smiled. "Not."

"Sit and relax, hon." He lifted Emma from his shoulders and cradled her in his arms. "I'll take Emma to her new room and tuck her into her new big girl bed."

"I'm a big girl," Emma babbled as Pete carried her into the house.

"At least the beds are set up. So much else to do." Wendy sighed. "What did you mean by bad cats, Mr. Harper?"

"There's feral cats in those woods. It's dangerous for a little one."

Wendy frowned. "The real estate agent never said anything about feral cats." She gathered up the used paper plates and napkins.

"Here, let me take that." Jim carried the trash to a plastic can. An image of Dora's gnawed fingers flashed in his mind and he tossed the skinny piece of chewed crust he held into the trash.

Wendy eased herself back into a chair. "You say these cats are dangerous? How?"

He hated to frighten a pregnant woman but feared for Emma's safety as well as for Wendy and her soon-to-be-born baby. "They're wild animals . . . could have rabies, disease, that sort of thing." He scanned the dark woodsy perimeter of the yard. One glowing green eye leered back from the underbrush.

"Is that what those traps are for? Pete thought they might be for raccoons."

Jim's breath caught in his throat as he stared over Wendy's head. The woods behind her glittered with dozens of shiny, almond-shaped eyes. "Uh, yes. Not to worry, they'll catch Inky, er, the cats."

"What's wrong?" Wendy struggled to turn her body in the chair. She pushed herself up, stood and looked where Jim stared. The eyes had disappeared into the blackness. "Do you see something, Mr. Harper?"

"Um, no. But please, keep Emma away from the woods." He started across the lawn, then stopped and turned. "Thank you, Wendy, and thank Pete too, for the pizza and the company. Welcome to the neighborhood."

Jim walked across the street, glancing at the empty animal control cages as he passed and then hurried into his house. He went to his closet, rummaged through what little he'd kept of his hunting gear and pulled out a pair of night vision binoculars.

After flicking off the porch light, he crept over to his rocking chair and eased himself into it. Holding the binoculars to his eyes, he adjusted the lenses and slowly scanned the expanse of woods to the side and behind Pete and Wendy's yard.

"You better not be peeping at my wife and daughter."

Jim gasped and dropped the binoculars. They clattered on the wooden porch floor.

A small orange dot glowed in the darkness at the base of his porch. As Jim's eyes adjusted, he made out Pete's hulking form standing at the foot of the porch steps. A lit cigarette hung from his lips.

"Pete. Jesus, you scared me. No, of course not. I-I watch for owls sometimes. A hobby."

"Yeah, well maybe you should give up your hobby until we get our drapes up."

Pete's tone and ugly insinuation angered Jim. He stood. "Listen here, I don't peep into people's houses. If you must know, I'm concerned about those feral cats. I spotted some in the woods when Emma ran off tonight."

"So owl watching was a lie?" Pete snorted. "Yeah, Wendy told me. You scared her. Keep your damn cat stories to yourself. I don't need you upsetting my pregnant wife. You hear me?"

Pete strode off before Jim could answer. A door slammed and the Driscols' front entry light flicked off.

Jim bent down and retrieved his binoculars. As he turned to go inside, he saw the pruners on the rail and remembered the cuttings he had left on his path. He hung the pruners up and started down the steps to scoop up the rose debris. A low growl coming from the depths of the dense jasmine bushes to his left made him stop and freeze in place on the bottom step.

Inky slunk out from beneath the bushes and hunched down on the walkway, his body low, long neck stretched out and mouth open. Muscles rippled along the length of its taunt body as the cat made a series of hacking coughs. Finally, it let out a loud retching sound. A slimy lump spat from its mouth and splattered onto the cement walk next to the rose cuttings. The cat glared up at Jim and then ran off toward the woods.

"Damn disgusting cats. Pissing, shitting and now puking all over my yard."

Jim climbed up the steps, switched on his porch light and leaned over the railing to examine the dark puddle on his walkway. In the midst of the spreading slime, a pale blue eyeball stared up at him. He staggered backward and fumbled with the doorknob and then backed into the house.

Minutes later, he returned armed with a handful of paper towels. Try as he might, Jim couldn't bring himself to pick up the eyeball. He mumbled an apology to both God and Dora as he retreated into his house, leaving the pale lifeless orb gazing up at the moonlit sky.

The disturbing image burned deep into his brain and wouldn't allow sleep to extinguish it. Jim spent the night prowling the house, listening for sounds and peeking out windows.

***

Just before sunrise, he gulped down a cup of too-hot coffee and then retrieved a spade from his shed. He scooped up dirt and mulch from the rose garden and covered the slimy mess on his front walkway.

Across the street an engine rumbled to life. He turned. Wendy stood on her front stoop waving to Pete as he backed the big truck down the driveway. Jim waved. Pete stopped and stared at him, letting the truck idle for a good thirty seconds before slowly rolling away. Wendy clutched the neckline of her bathrobe, ducked her head and slipped inside her front door.

"I've got to straighten things out with those two. Can't believe he thinks I'm a damn Peeping Tom." Jim gritted his teeth as he scraped the shovel along the cement and underneath the pile of dirt concealing the eyeball. He dumped the shovelful under the rose bushes and patted it down with the back of the spade.

After getting a second mug of coffee, he sat in his rocker and forced the image of the eyeball from his mind. The sun had risen and light washed over the east-facing porch. A warm breeze and the sound of birds chirping calmed him. He hadn't heard that many birds in years. Perhaps it was a sign that the cats had finally moved on. With poor old Dora dead, there was no one to feed the mangy beggars. He sipped his coffee and listened to the excited bird chatter growing in his back yard. No doubt they were enjoying the cool water in the birdbath under the morning sun.

***

As he walked the spade back to the shed, he noted spots of mulch in the grass that had been dug out from the flower beds and flung into the grass. "Damned cats."

A brown-and-white fluffy ball tucked into the grass in his back yard caught his attention. It wasn't mulch. He stooped to look closer and discovered a headless, dead sparrow. Bright red stained the white downy feathers of its belly. Its mangled head lay a few inches away.

"Poor bird. Must have flown into something and broke its neck. Never seen one snap it's head clear off before." He shuddered as he looked into its tiny blank eyes. An eerie silence had replaced the bird chatter.

He walked to his shed, hung up the spade and donned his work gloves. Grabbing a trash bag, he scooped up the dead bird parts with gloved hands and dropped them into the bag.

Feathers fluttered across the lawn in the morning breeze, too many for the one bird. He walked to the center garden, where the feathers were most concentrated. Six dead sparrow bodies, along with their severed heads, floated in the birdbath, the water red with blood. A dozen or more decapitated birds lay strewn about the garden beneath the bath.

"Jesus." The sight made him step back. It had to be the cats, or *the* cat. A chill jangled down his spine and his scalp prickled despite the hot sun. He swiveled his head from side to side, scanning his yard for any sign of Inky.

Plucking the tiny, sodden bodies from the water sickened him. No matter how lightly he tried to scoop them up, their fragile broken bodies squished between his fingers and bits of bloody tissue and feathers stuck to his gloves. Blood-red water and feathers cascaded over the edge of the basin when he rinsed it with the hose. Puffs of steam laced with the coppery smell of blood rose from the wet, sunbaked ground. Tying the plastic bag closed, he walked it to the trash can. The tiny, waterlogged bodies weighed heavy in his hand. He eased the bag into the trash can and pressed the lid down tight.

The grass needed cutting and the gardens needed weeding but cleaning up the bloody bird carnage had left him feeling nauseous and shaky. He trudged into the house and lay down on his bed.

The cats savaged those poor birds. He could still smell the blood and feel the soggy, mangled bodies in his hand. And the misunderstanding with the Driscols weighed on his mind. Should he tell Pete about Dora? The deputies theorized Dora died from natural causes and the cats did their damage after the fact. Jim wasn't convinced and it would take weeks for the autopsy results to learn the truth. Maybe he should dig up that dreadful blue eyeball and show it to Pete. Or show him the trash bag filled with massacred birds. Then he'd understand.

Jim's ears buzzed. Lack of sleep combined with the oppressive heat brought on a wave of dizziness. Sweat coated his face and body and his stomach pitched a steady stream of acid into the back of his throat. He had flipped off the air conditioner when he went outside like he always did. Rather than sit up and risk losing the volatile mix of coffee and bile in his stomach, he lay still and stared out the window.

"Damned cats. Especially that Inky." They had mauled little Justin, probably the reason why the Murrays packed up and moved so abruptly. Then Conrads only stayed less than two years. Wonder why? They had seemed happy enough with the house. Did the cats chew the wires and cause the fire in Bill Fuke's house? Jim never considered it before, but after what the cats did to Dora, anything was possible.

***

He awoke drenched in sweat, lying on his back atop the worn chenille bedspread just as he'd lain down. Glancing at the clock, the five-forty-five time and weak grayish light in his east window confused him. He pushed himself up and dangled his legs over the side of the bed until the fog lifted from his mind and he realized he had slept clear through the night.

Once he showered and dressed, he found his appetite and fixed himself a plate of scrambled eggs and toast. He regained his stamina by his second cup of coffee. Not quite seven o'clock, he'd get an early start in the yard before the heat set in and make up for the day he'd slept away. Sleep and the hearty breakfast invigorated him. He headed out to the shed and grabbed a leaf rake to clean up the scattered mulch and any other yard debris before mowing the grass.

The rake tines scraped against something hard, round and white protruding from beneath the marigolds bordering the center garden. He bent down and poked a gloved finger at the object. It rolled across the grass, bumped the toe of his shoe and came to rest with Chauncey's painted eyes gazing up at him. A few feet away, the gnome's body lay prone by the rhododendron. Deep claw marks scarred his painted vest and knickers.

He gently picked up Chauncey, both pieces, and carried him into the screen room. He placed the statue on his worktable, put on his glasses and examined the break. Jagged, but Super Glue might do the job. He'd putty the deeper gouges, then search through Tammy's bin of acrylic paints and attempt to touch up the gnome's face and body. Tammy would have been heartbroken. The sight enraged him.

Throwing a work towel over the devastated gnome, he walked outside to finish raking. He usually found the chore relaxing, but today his mind whirred with thoughts of feral cats.

"I'm not going to be outsmarted by a goddamn cat."

A flash of black ran across the yard toward the birdbath.

"You ballsy little bastard." Jim sprinted to the shed,

grabbed the spade and stomped over to the birdbath. Morning shadows sprawled across the yard. A light breeze ruffled the trees and shrubs. He spun around, scanning the moving leafy patterns of light and shadow.

A green eye glowed from the blackness under the hibiscus. Jim crept toward it. As he raised the spade to strike, the eye vanished. He caught movement from the corner of his eye and whirled around. Inky's lanky body sprang out from the shadow of the cypress tree. The cat darted across the yard, clearing the fence in one leap. Leaves rustled in Dora's yard, then quiet.

"I'm gonna kill you, you mangy black devil!" Jim banged the spade head against the wooden fence. "I'll kill all your damn offspring, too! Nine times each, if I have to."

Pete and Wendy strolled along the cul-de-sac, passing by Dora's house. Pete looked at Jim, shook his head and then draped a protective arm around Wendy's shoulders. The two turned, picked up their pace and headed back toward their house.

Jim let out a long sigh and leaned the spade against the fence. He trudged across the yard and resumed raking. He waited until he heard Pete's truck rumble away before raking the front yard.

Raking led to weeding and then edging the front flower beds. The sun shone hot overhead by the time Jim decided to break for lunch. He settled into his recliner and ate a ham and cheese on rye. The disgusted expression on

Pete's face played in his mind, and even worse, the look of fear on Wendy's. He had to apologize to Wendy. He wished for the thousandth time that Tammy were here. Everyone loved Tammy. She had a way with people. She'd smooth things over with her sweet smile and a homemade peach cobbler. But Tammy was gone. He'd have to bumble his way through an apology on his own and hopefully not upset the poor woman any more than he already had.

Emma's happy shrieks rang out across the street. Jim peeked through his blinds. The little girl kicked a bright yellow ball around her front lawn. Wendy poked her head out the open front door and cautioned her daughter to stay near the house. The little girl obliged, changing direction and kicking the ball toward the house.

Taking a deep breath, Jim stepped out on his front porch and walked down the three steps. "Keep it simple," he muttered. "Mrs. Driscol, I apologize. There's been a misunderstanding—" Jim's thoughts froze, and his heart skipped a beat. Emma stood at the edge of the woods. She crouched, peered into the thick foliage and called, "Hi, kiddy. Hi, kiddy. Wanna play?"

As he ran across the street, he glanced over at the Driscols' front door. Wendy was nowhere in sight. Emma dropped down on all fours and crawled into the brush.

"No, sweetheart. Stay away from that cat!" he shouted.

Emma squeezed deeper into the brush, her blonde ponytails tangling in the low-hanging branches.

Jim jogged the last few steps, swooped his arms around Emma's waist and pulled her from the underbrush.

The little girl shrieked, flailed her arms and kicked her legs. "Leggo! Leggo! Mommy!"

Wendy screamed, "Emma!"

Jim spun around keeping a tight grasp on the squirming girl.

"You put her down!" Wendy ran across the grass as best she could hugging her pregnant belly.

Jim gently placed Emma down on the ground. In her struggle to get away, she tripped and fell face down in the grass. Her shrill shrieks turned to tearful howls.

"It's okay. Don't cry, Emma." Jim bent to help the child to her feet.

"Don't you touch her!" Wendy slapped his hands away as she dropped to her knees and cradled Emma in her arms. "Get away! Go!"

Jim shuffled backward until his heels hit the pavement of the road. "I'm sorry. I didn't mean to scare—I was afraid the cat . . . I'm so sorry."

The little girl's hiccupping cries drowned out Jim's apology. Wendy struggled to her feet, hauled Emma onto her hip and hurried into the house. She slammed the front door.

The bright yellow ball lay at the edge of the woods. Inches away a green eye glinted in the darkness and then vanished.

Three loud bangs on his front door made Jim jump. His trembling hands sloshed water from his glass as he set it on the kitchen table. He opened the door, surprised to see the young deputy standing there.

"Deputy Rollins. Do you have news about Dora?"

The young man shook his head. "No, Mr. Harper. I'm here to talk to you. Got a complaint from Mrs. Driscol across the way. A serious one. She says you molested her little girl this afternoon."

"M-Molested? No! No, this is all a misunderstanding. Emma crawled into the woods. I saw that damn cat, Inky—" The sound of a loud engine interrupted. The deputy turned toward the street.

Pete's big black truck lurched to a stop in front of Jim's house. He jumped out, leaving the driver's door open and engine running. "You sick son of a bitch!" He stormed up Jim's path.

"Stop right there, sir." Deputy Rollins headed off Pete at the foot of the stairs. Another deputy came jogging from across the street and stood next to Rollins.

"What is your name, sir?" Rollins asked.

"Pete Driscol. Emma's father. My wife called you about this old pervert grabbing our daughter."

"Now you hold on, Pete," Jim said. "I'd never hurt Emma or any child. I was only trying to keep her from getting scratched or bit by that cat."

"Cat? Here we go again with the freaking cats. You're not only a pervert, but a goddamn whack job, too!"

"Mr. Driscol, I need you to go to your home. Let me speak to Mr. Harper," Rollins said. The second deputy placed his hand on Pete's shoulder. Pete shrugged it off and took a step forward.

The deputy gripped Pete's arm. "Mr. Driscol, come with me. Don't make this situation any worse."

"Pete!" Wendy crossed the road, face pale, eyes red and arms hugging her stomach.

Pete shook his fist at Jim but allowed the deputy to lead him toward the street. He slid his arm around Wendy's waist. As they walked toward their yard, his head swiveled to look back at Jim and Rollins. "This ain't over, you old fu—"

"That's enough, Mr. Driscol." The escorting deputy gave Pete a light push and the three walked to the Driscols' front yard. Emma ran to her father and he gathered her up in his arms.

Rollins turned back to Jim. "I understand that scene with Ms. Pritchard upset you—it's my fault. I should never have let you enter the house."

"Sergeant Monahan said those cats mauled the Murray boy. I was trying to protect that sweet little girl. I picked her up, took her away from the woods and put her down. I scared her and she tripped. I'm sorry for that, but damn it, Deputy, I'd do the same thing again if I saw one of those cats near her. My God, those damn devils killed poor old Dora."

"We have no proof the cats killed Dora Pritchard. Look Jim, I'm gonna cut you a break. Stay clear of the Driscols, especially their little girl. Hopefully this will all quiet down." Rollins sighed. "I'll go talk to Driscol, tell him it was a misunderstanding."

"But deputy—"

"Just let it be, Jim. You hear me? Now please, go inside your house and stay there."

***

That evening, Jim sat inside his back screened porch sipping a beer and tapping his foot. "Can't even sit on my own damned front porch. Ridiculous." He took a long swig of beer. He had to explain his actions to Wendy and Pete, although with the state Pete was in, there'd be no talking sense to him tonight.

He heard a noise in the back yard. Flipping on the floodlights, he stood inside the screen door and searched the yard. Inky strolled across the patch of lit grass.

"Damn bastard cat." He grabbed a broom and stormed into the yard. His foot landed on something hard. His ankle gave a dull pop and a sharp pain shot up his leg. He fell on his side.

"Shit." He pushed himself onto all fours and squinted at the strange, grayish-white object lying in the grass. His wrapped his fingers around it, thinking it was a large, odd-shaped rock. He'd raked the lawn this morning. There were no rocks. It took him three attempts to stand on his injured ankle. He held the object up to the light, gasped and dropped it. The rock had teeth. A jawbone, about the size of a dog's.

He limped on his hurt ankle to the far end of the yard to inspect his dog's grave site. The floodlights' glare ended at dog's grave. The stone plaque sat crooked and a pile of excrement covered Cody's name. Dark stains on the coquina boulder above it reeked of fresh urine. A hole had been dug out underneath one side of the plaque and white bones lay scattered in the grass.

Jim hobbled to the shed and retrieved his flashlight and spade. He limped around the yard with tears stinging his eyes, picked up Cody's bones with trembling hands and returned them to the dug-up grave. He covered the hole with the loose dirt and reset the plaque on top. Shoveling up the vile-smelling feces, he carried it to the fence and flung it into Dora's overgrown back yard.

After rinsing the plaque and boulder down with the hose, he hauled himself up the back porch steps on his throbbing ankle, exhausted and furious. Ignoring the pain, he tore through the cabinets under the kitchen sink searching for any kind of poison. Tammy had been dead set against them and wouldn't allow them in the house.

He vowed he'd go to Home Depot tomorrow and buy rat poison.

***

The swelling and pain in his ankle had worsened by the following morning. He found an ace bandage in the medicine cabinet and wrapped his ankle. It hurt to put his weight on the leg, and he abandoned the idea of going to Home Depot. He watched through his blinds until Pete's truck drove away before he ventured out onto his front porch. The animal control truck rolled past. The officer parked, hopped out of her truck and checked each of the traps.

Jim eased his way down the porch steps and limped to the end of his walkway. "Did you catch any black cats?" he asked.

"Caught something." The woman picked up two of the cages and slid them into the bed of her truck. Meows and snarls coming from inside the cages broke the morning quiet.

"Is it a black one with only one eye?"

The woman shook her head and waited while Jim shuffled his way over to the truck. He peeked into the cages. A gold and white tabby and the big gray male with tattered ears glared back at him.

"You gotta catch the big black one. One green eye. Inky. He's their ringleader."

The officer raised her eyebrows and grunted. She reset the remaining traps and then drove away.

Jim gimped back into his house, his ankle throbbing,

and dropped into his chair.

The sight of his overgrown lawn gnawed at him, but he couldn't handle the mower while hobbling on his painful ankle. He spent the day clicking the TV remote, his leg elevated in his recliner. None of the shows kept his attention. He dozed off and on, but the brief naps brought nightmares of Dora's mangled corpse, the horrid eyeball, mangled birds and Emma running in her yard, her tiny face a bloody mask.

***

Jim's entire weekly routine had been ruined. Evenings were no longer a peaceful interlude to enjoy a beer on his front porch. The injured ankle prevented him from doing yard work. After napping most of the day he lay awake in bed at night or limped from window to window to investigate any strange noises.

Tired of being banished from his own front porch, Jim waited until after Pete Driscol's truck pulled up and he heard their front door close. Leaving his porch light off, Jim sneaked out to his rocking chair clutching a beer. He sat still and rigid in the chair, scanning the cul-de-sac. His body tensed at each frog chirp and the occasional owl hoot. Finding no relaxation, he gulped down his beer and then crept back into the house.

His ankle still ached the following Saturday morning and he called Bill early to beg off going fishing. He told Bill he'd sprained an ankle while working in the yard but left out the part about Cody's ravaged grave and the scattered bones.

***

Every morning after Pete left for work, Jim rushed to his porch railing and waited like a kid for Christmas while the animal control officer checked the traps. She called out the color of any captured cats. So far only five had been caught, none of them black cats.

The third morning she waved to Jim. "Got a black one. Looks like only one eye, too."

Jim's heart raced. He set his coffee mug on the porch railing and hurried as best he could on his tender ankle. He bent to inspect the cage in the truck bed. A jet-black face with one greenish-yellow eye stared back. His heartbeat sped up. "You got the little bas–"

The cat clawed at the metal bars of the cage with two white paws. Then he saw the third white paw on her hind leg. It was the female cat Dora had named Three Socks.

On closer inspection, one of the cat's eyes was only partially closed and oozed a yellowish pus. "Dammit."

"Not the one?" the woman asked.

"No, it's not Inky." Jim let out a long sigh. "Well, maybe tomorrow."

She slid empty cages into the truck. "Won't be here tomorrow. Ten days is our limit. You can call again if you see more cats and we'll come back out."

"But there's at least forty cats, you've only caught,

what, six? What about the rest?"

"It's six more ferals off the streets. This is a small township, we have limited resources and lots of animal complaints."

***

The swelling in his ankle finally subsided and the sight of his shaggy grass irked Jim into action. He made his way to the shed, determined to pull out the mower and at least cut the front lawn. As he neared the shed, he noticed the door stood ajar. He mustn't have latched it in his upset the night he discovered Cody's desecrated grave.

Sunlight poured into the shed as he pulled open the door. A loud snarl startled him. In the back left corner stood a black cat with its back hunched and ears flattened. This cat was too small and slightly built to be Inky. He stepped closer and saw movement behind the cat. A wriggling pile of kittens nested in the crate of old bedsheets he used to cover the plants in case of a frost. One struggled to stand on its shaky legs. The pure black kitten rested its head on the edge of the crate. It only had one eye.

The mother cat hissed and then let out a low growl that grew into a raspy wail.

Jim plucked a rake from a hook and waved it at the cat. "Shoo! Get out" Once he could get to the kittens, he'd bundle them up and take them to Dora's yard, then call animal control to come and take them away. The she-cat sprung. The rake tines glanced off her body as she swiped her front claws down Jim's bare shins, then she whipped around and resumed her defensive stance in front of her brood.

"Shit!" Jim flung the rake into the grass as he backed out of the shed and inspected his bleeding legs. He turned and headed for the hose.

Inky sat calmly licking his front paw next to the coiled hose.

Jim hesitated, wondering if he should go back and grab the rake. Anger prodded him forward.

"Get! Damn cat! Get out of here!" He waved his arms and stamped his feet.

Inky dashed past Jim and slipped inside the open shed.

Jim turned on the spigot, snatched up the nozzle end of the hose and chased after him. Wincing at the thought of soaking all of his tools, he aimed the hose into the shed and turned the nozzle to full blast. No water came out.

"Shit!"

He turned. Tiny spouts of water squirted upward from needle-sized punctures that riddled the entire length of the hose.

"Goddamn devil of an animal. My hose is ruined." He rubbed his hands over his sweaty face as he scanned the gardens of wilting plants and drooping flowers. His ankle throbbed from stamping his foot.

Jim hobbled up his back steps into the house and called animal control. He'd have them remove the litter of kittens and set up traps in his back yard. A long-winded recording stated office hours, spay and neutering information, and then finally a shrill tone sounded. A click interrupted just as Jim stated his name and address, then a dial tone buzzed. He re-dialed, sat through the recording and as he began his message, the dial tone cut him off again. He slammed the phone down on the kitchen counter.

***

Exhausted, Jim tossed in his bed, unable to sleep that night. The sorry state of his yard and the uneasy situation with his new neighbors plagued him. Although both bedroom windows were wide open, there was no breeze. Humidity hung in the still night air like a steamy cloud, yet there was no sign of rain. Rain would do his gardens good. Unless he toted dozens of watering cans back and forth from the spigot, rain would be the only source of water the plants would have until he could afford a new hose.

He shuffled numbers in his head. If he kept the air conditioner off and cut off the cable for a month or two, he'd save enough money to buy both the roll of wire mesh and a hose. But what if that bastard of a cat chewed and clawed the new hose? He needed a permanent solution. There would be no peace until he got rid of the cats once and for all. Animal control had proven useless. Inky was too smart to be lured into their traps. Tomorrow he'd go out and buy the rat poison. With a plan in place, he closed his eyes.

A metallic scraping noise jarred him from his twilight daze. He sat up in bed. Claws raked at his bedroom window screen.

"Mother of God!" He stood, his heartbeat pounding in his ears, and turned on the lamp on the bedside table. The light reflected on a green eye shimming in the blackness outside the window screen.

"Get!" He grabbed his bed pillow and flung it at the window. The pillow snagged and then tore on the jagged cut in the screen when he pulled it back. Clumps of foam stuffing cascaded to the floor. An image of Inky, licking his bloody paw before slipping out Dora's slashed bedroom window screen flashed in his mind.

Chills raced down his spine even as sweat dripped from his forehead. He slammed the window shut. A low growl sounded and then branches scraped against the other window screen. He ran across the room, closed it and locked it.

He ran through the house, from window to window, making sure they were all shut tight and locked. Shadowy shapes lurked on the outside sills and hunched in nearby tree branches. The porch light outlined sleek silhouettes perched on the railing outside the drawn living room blinds. Claws tugged at the screens. Long, plaintive wails rose from his back yard.

He hunkered in his recliner as the cats clawed at his screens, the noise amplified in the quiet night. He almost called the sheriff, but they would think him a fool. A grown man complaining about a bunch of stray cats. Plus, he'd had enough attention from the deputies lately.

Loud ripping noises came from the back screened porch. He stood with his hand on the back doorknob. If he opened the door to chase them, they might run into the house. He retreated to his recliner and listened. After what seemed like hours, the noises stopped.

Jim let out a long breath and leaned back in his chair. The heat made him weary and lethargic, but he had to leave the air conditioner off to save money.

Footsteps scampered overhead. He stared up at the ceiling. They were on the roof, scratching at the shingles. What if they managed to claw open a vent? He rushed from room to room feeling the walls above the outlets and sniffing the air for any hint of smoke.

***

Jim didn't take time to shower or shave. He pulled on his clothes at first light and drove to Home Depot. He returned two hours later, the back of his SUV loaded with rolls of heavy wire mesh and boxes of nails. The cost of the materials plus the two large plastic bags of rat poison pellets had put a good-sized dent in his checking account. He'd cancel his cable and keep his air conditioning off until he recouped the money spent.

Jim inspected the tattered screens on the front windows and then walked around to the back screened porch. He gasped at the long slashes and jagged rips. Mangled sheets of screen dangled from the aluminum framework. The porch reeked of urine. Chauncey lay shattered on the tile floor, too many tiny pieces to glue back together. The only thing that hadn't been torn up was the new reinforced mesh panel he'd installed.

Before attempting to enter his tool shed, he searched the house for something—anything—to protect himself from the feral cat's attacks. He donned his old catcher's mask he'd kept from when he played on his post office baseball team. He cut up the empty milk jugs in his recycling bin and fashioned shin guards, then wound thick vinyl floral place mats he found in the kitchen pantry around his forearms. He secured the place mats and plastic jugs to his arms and legs with lengths of duct tape. Then he entered the shed. The mother cat attacked as he reached for a ladder, but her claws skidded on the smooth plastic milk jug rather than digging into his flesh. He pulled the ladder out, and without bothering to remove his gear, set to work.

The rolls of stiff mesh were unwieldy to manage and his wire cutters dull. Jim didn't stop and waste precious time to sharpen them. The blades chewed at the wire as he hacked off uneven swatches. He nailed two pieces crisscrossed over each of the back windows, then wrapped rolls of mesh around the screen room and used zip ties and nylon cord to fasten it to the metal framework. It looked sloppy, but secure.

He dragged the ladder from window to window, its feet crushing plants and shrubs, as he set it down into the flower beds and climbed up to nail the wire mesh to the decorative wooden shutters. Time, weather and several coats of paint had hardened the wood. The nails bent and some snapped. He pulled more from his pockets and kept pounding until enough stayed in the wood to secure the mesh.

Pete's oversized truck ambled into his driveway as Jim hammered the mesh across one side of his double front windows. Pete walked to the sidewalk in front of his house and stared. "What the hell . . . a catcher's mask? You are nuts."

Jim ignored him and focused on pounding in nails. In his haste to finish before sunset, his wild swings missed the nail heads and struck the block wall. Chinks of painted cement rained down onto the porch. His arm ached from swinging the hammer. The last blow missed its mark entirely and shattered his front window.

"Crazy old fool." Pete shouted. He turned, shook his head, entered his house and slammed his front door.

With no money to buy plywood, Jim broke apart a wooden shelving unit in the laundry room and hammered the slats across the front window. House secured, he turned his focus to the rat poison.

For good measure he mixed the poison pellets in a large bucket with several cans of tuna he had in his pantry.

By nightfall, he finished spreading the mixture around his yard. Easing open the shed door, he threw a handful into the dark space. Snarls, growls and the mews of the kittens rang out from the darkness. From the volume, it sounded as though more cats had taken up residence inside.

***

He dropped exhausted into his rocking chair on the front porch clutching a bottle of beer. His bloodied arms and shins stung from peeling off the duct tape, along with ample amounts of body hair and skin in the process. The full moon's light shone on the white pellets scattered over his overgrown lawn and withered flower beds. The warm breeze carried the fishy smell.

He had moved the chair to the darkest corner of the porch and ducked down behind the thick rose bushes to avoid Pete's attention.

Jim thought about calling Bill to tell him he wouldn't be going fishing again tomorrow morning, but after securing the house, he felt better. He looked forward to getting back into his normal routine, especially a peaceful day of fishing at the lake. He downed two aspirins with a sip of beer to soothe his sore muscles and rocked on his front porch.

"Better hit the sack. Gotta be up early." A loud clanging noise made him jump as he pushed himself up from the rocker.

Dora's metal trash can rolled down her driveway,

bumped over the curb and wobbled into the road. The lid fell off and clattered on the blacktop. His heart pounding from the scare, Jim leaned over the railing to look. Inky strode down Dora's driveway. The cat stood next to the empty trash can and yowled.

Jim dropped his beer bottle and grabbed the hammer.

"Get out of here! Scat!" He edged down the steps to the end of his walkway waving the hammer.

The Driscols' front light flicked on. Pete carried a small suitcase out to the blue sedan. "What the hell are you yelling about now?"

Jim turned toward Pete. "It's that cat, Inky. Knocked over the trash can."

"I don't see any goddamn cat. Crazy old drunk."

Jim scanned the dark road. Inky had disappeared.

"Pete, hurry, please." Wendy slowly made her way to the car. "The pains are coming closer."

"Okay, honey." He helped Wendy into the passenger seat. "C'mon, Emma. Let's go." Emma ran to the car, clutching a pink backpack, and climbed into the back seat. Pete locked the front door, then jogged to the car. He backed the car down the driveway and sped off.

Jim would have liked to wish Wendy well, but, under the circumstances, all he could do was stand and watch them drive off.

As soon as the sedan disappeared from his sight, the woods at the end of the cul-de-sac rustled to life. Cats emerged from the underbrush like a murky, liquid stain seeping across the road and swelling in size as they approached Jim's house. Inky led the pack.

Jim stood staring, mouth agape. "My God, there's more. Must be a hundred of them." He backed up his porch steps, brandishing the hammer in front of him.

Inky stopped at the foot of Jim's front walk. The swarm behind him stopped, raised their heads and let out a deafening cacophony of wails, howls and shrieks.

Jim dropped the hammer and grasped the front doorknob. He slid inside, slamming the door behind him, and ran to his bedroom closet. He pulled out his pellet gun. For the first time in his life, he cursed Tammy for making him sell his semi-automatic hunting rifle. But, the .22 air gun could easily take out a cat. He checked the scope and grabbed a box of the heaviest pellets he had on the shelf. Though the heavier pellet assured a straighter shot, he could only load one at a time. If his aim held true, he only needed only one shot—right in Inky's damn green eye.

He pressed his ear to the front door. Silence. Opening it a crack, he peered outside. The mob of howling cats had vanished. Only Inky sat, mid-way down his front walk, staring up at him.

A perfect target. Jim eased out the front door and crept out onto the porch, watching the cat through the scope of the gun.

"Stay right there, you evil little bastard." Jim squinted

as he aimed. The vertical crosshair lined up perfectly with Inky's black slit of a pupil.

Holding his breath to keep the gun steady, Jim couldn't help but grin. "Guess you ain't such a smart cat after all."

Razor sharp claws ripped into his back and shoulders. Cats leaped on him from all directions. They hung on with their claws and sunk their teeth into his flesh. Jim staggered backwards, batting the animals away with the gun barrel. More raced up the porch steps and others jumped from tree branches. Claws slashed his face, arms, chest, back and legs. The open box of ammo fell from his pocket and dozens of pellets bounced on the wooden porch floor. Needle-like fangs punctured his calves and ankles. He kicked at the frenzied swarm of bodies surrounding him on the porch. His blows sent wiry bodies flying through air, but they landed on calloused pads and doubled back to attack again. Pellets skittled across the wooden porch. Jim slipped and skidded on the rolling metal projectiles. He tumbled backwards down the three front steps and landed on his back. His head banged into the cement walkway. His vision blurred, either from the hard blow to the back of his head or the blood streaming into his eyes.

※ ※ ※

The Driscol house was quiet Saturday morning. Wendy and Pete hadn't returned home yet with their newborn son. Jim sat quietly rocking on the porch holding a mug of hot coffee when Bill drove up at six o'clock sharp.

"All set?" Bill called from the driver's window.

"Sorry, Bill, I meant to call you. I'm gonna pass on fishing today."

"Again?" Bill climbed from the truck, engine running. "Good Lord, Jim! What the hell happened to you? And your house?"

"Looks worse than it is. Took a tumble off the ladder while I was cleaning out the gutters. Landed in the rose bushes." He pointed to the thicket of roses in front of the porch. "Ladder busted the window."

"Want me to drive you to the clinic? You're cut up pretty bad, especially your right eye."

"Nah, I'll be all right. I scrubbed with peroxide."

Bill hesitated at the bottom porch step. "Should I stop by and check on you later?"

"No need, but thank you. Go catch the big one, Bill. I'm gonna rest-up here today."

Bill's nose wrinkled. "What stinks?" His head swiveled from Jim to the mesh-covered windows and then to the high grass littered with white pellets and hunks of rancid tuna baking in the morning sun. He looked up at Jim. "What's going on—are you sure you're feeling all right, Jim?"

"Yup, just a little sore. You go on now, I'll be fine." He waved for Bill to leave.

Bill stood for a moment with his mouth open and

shaking his head. "Call me if you need anything, you hear?" He slid into his truck and backed down the drive. He cruised around the bend of the cul-de-sac and drove off.

Jim finished his coffee and carried the mug into the kitchen. He emptied the contents of his fishing fund jar onto the countertop and counted it. A light windbreaker and jeans covered the scratches, bites and gouges on his arms and legs. He looked a sight with Band-aids plastered over the deeper wounds on his face. An eye patch left over from his cataract surgery shielded his scratched right eye. Bloody spikes of matted hair stuck out at odd angles on the back of his head where he had cut it when he fell and gray hair curled over his ears and down the back of his neck. With all the commotion, he'd missed his monthly trip to the barber shop. He had no money for a haircut anyway. His beard looked scruffy as well, but shaving wasn't an option until the cuts and gashes on his face healed.

He pocketed the fishing fund money, locked up the house, and then climbed into his Honda SUV. Jim didn't like lying to Bill, but it was easier than explaining what he had to do.

***

Sunset came just before eight o'clock that evening. Jim put his empty beer bottle down next to the others lined up on the porch floor. He walked down the steps and opened the rear hatch of his Honda. The underbrush at the end of the cul-de-sac bustled with activity. The mewing grew louder.

Jim was ready for the cats tonight. He had everything he needed in the car. His muscles ached and the scratches and bites throbbed, but he forced himself to hurry before the horde arrived.

Across the street, the Driscols' porch light flicked on. The blue sedan sat parked in the driveway. Pete yelled something, but the rising din of the approaching cats drowned out his words.

The clomp of Pete's heavy boots on the road drew closer. He stopped at the curb in front of Jim's house. "I asked you what the hell you're doing, you crazy old bastard."

Jim carried a twenty-pound bag to the end of his fence line, ripped it open and then slowly shuffled backwards, dumping dry cat food along the sidewalk in front of his house.

Shaking the last nuggets from the bag, Jim winked at Pete with his unbandaged left eye.

"It's my turn now. Have to feed the cats."

He shuffled to his car and retrieved another bag.

Coming soon from Chris Holmes
and Paranormalice Press, LLC:

Inky II

Thorn of Roses (A Novel)

PARANOR**M**ALI**Œ**
PRESS, LLC

If you enjoyed this read, make the author happy by writing
a review on Amazon or Goodreads.

For questions or comments:
paranormalicepress@gmail.com

visit us at: www.paranormalicepress.com